THE DOUBLE
Rainbow

Mazi McBurnie

BALBOA.PRESS

A DIVISION OF HAY HOUSE

Balboa Press books may be ordered through booksellers or by contacting:

Balboa Press
A Division of Hay House
1663 Liberty Drive
Bloomington, IN 47403
www.balboapress.com.au
1 (877) 407-4847

Print information available on the last page.

ISBN: 978-1-5043-2153-2 (sc)
ISBN: 978-1-5043-2152-5 (e)

Balboa Press rev. date: 05/22/2020

DEDICATION

FOR JUANITA

CONTENTS

SYNOPSIS

"*The Double Rainbow*" *follows the story of Molly Duffy, who at age sixteen* was sentenced to seven years transportation to Australia, for stealing a packet of oats. Molly's story is one of courage and positivity as she struggles through tragedy and hardship to go from being a poor convict to become one of Australia's wealthiest women.

Leaving her family at home in England, with her father dying, Molly faces an unknown environment in a strange land. Her ability to cope with many hardships and her determination to retain her dignity in spite of all opposition, leads the reader to relate to the character of Molly in an empathetic way, hoping as she does for better things and a brighter future.

After reading Molly's story you will all agree that Molly is a woman of inspiration to others. Her caring nature and courageous actions make her a character whom you will enjoy following, through the pages of the novel, keen to change the page to meet the next exciting event in Molly's life.

C H A P T E R

1

Melbourne – Australia
(Circa 1840)

The ship had docked in Melbourne, after a rough journey around the Cape with many people ill and some overboard, Storms, terrifying at times were many and passengers both free settlers and convicts as well, were thrown like bags of garbage across the rough wooden floors of the ship "Navorina". The "Navorina" was home for months to free settlers, officers and many convicts on their way to Australia to serve out their sentences as deemed appropriate by the British Law Courts.

The free settlers and officers had left the ship by now and the convicts stood huddled together on a bare patch of grass, all with long, dirty, dank hair. Their hair was now greasy and unwashed for months, along with filthy clothing as they stood in a group waiting to be collected. They would then be handed over to their new masters to serve out their time in varied lengths of years. Some were short terms of five or seven years, but others were for life. It was difficult to tell who were the women and who were men, as they all looked the same and each one had a look of complete despair on their face. It was clear on their faces that each one of them had lost all dignity and hope.

One such person was young Molly Duffy, aged seventeen, from inner London, separated from her mother, father and older brother Philip for the first time in her young life. Molly had been sentenced to seven years transportation to Australia for the minor theft of a small bag of oats. She appeared before a magistrate in a London court and was sentenced just a few months ago. After sentencing, Molly was then taken to a women's prison to await transportation on the next ship going to Australia.

Molly was a sweet, gentle girl with a loving, giving nature, who in an act of desperation picked up a bag of oats and walked out of the store without paying for them. The shopkeeper who had known Molly and her family for many years, decided to call the police in spite of Molly's pleas and before she knew it, a policeman came and reluctantly took Molly away. "Please, please, Mr Young, I will pay you next week when I get paid," said Molly tearfully. The shopkeeper replied, "If I let you go, I will have all of you "down and outs" coming in here to steal. I have to send you paupers a message, once and for all."

Molly's father had been an accountant, but a lung disease had meant that he could no longer work to support his family. Her mother Sarah Duffy was a dressmaker, but only received minimal work, while Molly worked as a scullery maid in one of the big fancy houses in the village in which they lived. The Duffy's had a disabled son named Philip who was a gentle boy, but unable to work.

Recently Molly had taken to going through the rubbish bins from the big house where she worked. This was the only food that the Duffy's had to eat. All of Molly's small wage and the tiny income from her mother's sewing, went to pay for medicine to keep Ben Duffy alive.

Molly's time at the women's prison was horrendous. She was bullied and beaten on a daily basis. Her food was stolen and she was frequently in the prison hospital with broken bones. The nurses kept her there longer than necessary in order for her to get fed, taking pity on the sixteen year old girl. Some of the women were re-offenders and knew the ropes, picking on the younger and more vulnerable prisoners.

When Molly left the prison she was covered in a rainbow of bruises ranging from blue and black to now fading orange and yellow.

While Molly was at the women's prison, her father, Ben struggled to make the journey to the prison to visit her before she left for Australia. "Father, you must conserve your strength," she said. "My poor little girl, look at all of the bruises you have. How much you have endured, because of me," he said sadly. "Father, I would do anything for you, I love you so much," Molly replied.

"There is something I must tell you my dear. It is a matter which has weighed heavily upon me and one which I should have told you a long time ago," said Ben. "What is it father"? asked Molly, now curious. "Well, when you were born, you were born a twin," said Ben seriously. "A twin, how wonderful. What happened to my twin?" asked Molly.

"Your mother was not in a good way then dear, she was suffering from bad nerves and already had Philip whom we love dearly but is however a lot of work. The other little girl was very restless and colicky. She cried constantly and so we made the decision together to put her up for adoption. She went to a good home, we know that, and you were a perfect baby, never cried, always calm and placid. We do not regret the decision we made all those years ago, but I felt that you should know that you have a sister somewhere out there. I want no secrets between us now as you leave and I shall die in peace."

That was the last time Molly saw her father as he left, coughing and spluttering. She knew that he did not have long to live. Tears rolled down her beautiful face as she said goodbye.

C H A P T E R

2

The Convict

It was a beautiful summer day when the ship docked in Melbourne. The convicts began to disburse, going off to their new masters, not a clue as to where they were going or who their new masters would be. Molly shielded her eyes from the bright sun with her arm and looked up to see a sign which said Molly Duffy. She went over to the sign, held by a grumpy looking man and told him that she was Molly Duffy. He pointed to a coach and with a scowl on his face led Molly to the coach. Molly enjoyed the bumpy coach ride, keenly looking out of the small window at the distant sea and the beautiful Australian Gum trees. She was fascinated with the wild life, seeing kangaroos and koalas for the first time. Soon they arrived in Ballarat where Molly was to serve her sentence with a Mr and Mrs Penfield of "Seven Oaks". She had no knowledge of Ballarat, but one of the women on the ship had told her it was a gold mining town a few hours from Melbourne. The groom took Molly around the back entrance of a magnificent Manor house, worried that someone would see him with the convict.

Once at the back door, Molly was greeted by the housekeeper whose name was Mrs Beale. She was a middle aged woman with frizzy hair. She was firm but fair and had a good heart. Mrs Beale took Molly to the back sheds and took off her dirty clothes and threw them in the garbage bin. She heated water in a copper and washed her from top to toe, especially her hair which was greasy and dirty. Molly's hair was usually golden blonde and she had beautiful blue eyes. Mrs Beale then took Molly to her room where two uniforms in colour brown were laid out on the bed along with two white caps and two white aprons.

Molly squealed with delight when she saw her room. It was a small room, but had a cupboard for clothes and a window, a wash stand and an iron bed with a horsehair mattress and a soft pillow. On the bed was a patchwork quilt in shades of pink. Mrs Beale then left Molly and asked her to put on her uniform and report to her in the scullery. Molly was so excited to have a room of her own and such a pretty one at that. "Oh, Mrs Beale, this is the most beautiful room I have ever lived in, thank you so much," said Molly. To which Mrs Beale replied "You will work hard here my girl, so you need a decent night's rest."

Molly then went to the kitchen to meet the cook, Mrs Banks. Mrs Banks was a chubby woman with pinkish cheeks and a friendly smile. She could be fierce if crossed or if anyone came into her kitchen uninvited. Molly was given her list of tasks for each day. She was to rise at six am and get the fire going with wood from the pile outside. The night watchman filled the stove during the night so it would be ready for morning chores. Then when the water was hot she was to wash the floors of the kitchen and scullery and other outer areas. She then gathered wood to put on the pile as the fire needed to be kept going all day for hot water and cooking. Following these tasks she was to gather the eggs from the chook house.

After a good night's sleep when Molly had her best sleep in many months, Molly was woken at six am to start her chores on her first day. At around eight am, she was served breakfast in the little room off the scullery away from the other servants. She had oats and toast with honey and a pot of tea. Molly was grateful for the food as she was really hungry. The servant girl rushed in with the food and then ran from the room as if being chased by a herd of elephants. The other servants were curious to know more about the "convict". Eva asked "What is she like Tilly, does she have any hair?" "Of course she has hair, silly," replied Tilly. "Well I'm not going anywhere near her," said Eva.

Molly found the first few days tiring, as her body was so depleted through lack of food and the beatings she had endured over the past months. She was painfully thin and her uniform swam on her, but the large apron covered most of her. Her hair had not yet regained its lustre so she tied it into a tight bun at the top of her head and found an old pair of spectacles, which she used to cover her lovely deep blue eyes.

All in all, Molly was better off than she had been in London. At least she was well fed and had a lovely soft bed and pillow. The only thing concerning her, was her family back in England. She felt that her father would have died by now and worried as to how her mother Sarah, and brother Philip were managing without her small wage coming in. Molly had them constantly in her thoughts and prayed each night for them.

Molly coped with her tasks each day without complaint, impressing both Mrs Beale and Mrs Banks from day one. They could not understand how a lovely young girl with beautiful manners could have been convicted and transported for seven years.

Mrs Banks informed The Penfields about the arrival of the convict, but they were not interested. They agreed to take the convict thinking it would be a way to get cheap labour. After all, all they had to do was to feed her.

Luncheon on Molly's first day was boiled mutton with mustard sauce, followed by apple pie and boiled custard. Molly was thrilled with her meal and made a point of telling Mrs Banks how much she enjoyed it. "That was the nicest meal I have ever had in my life," said Molly. Mrs Banks smiled and thanked her. She later said to Mrs Beale, "That girl has been well brought up. I wonder why she became a convict?"

Molly still had her meals alone weeks and then months later. Gradually her body started to improve and she felt less tired. He figure started to change and she noticed a few curves starting to develop. The other servants still stayed away from her, but were no longer frightened that "the convict" would do them harm.

Molly spent most of her time washing and drying dishes from the three meals and peeling vegetables in the scullery. After about a year Mrs Banks allowed Molly into the kitchen to help with meal preparation. She loved working beside Mrs Banks who was a very experienced cook. Molly watched her carefully and took notes which she read at night to recall what she had done during the day. Although just a convict, Molly took her work very seriously and was keen to learn as much as she could.

"Seven Oaks" was a large house owned by the Penfield's who came to Australia about ten years ago and built the mansion, using convict labour. It was built of stone and mud bricks, was three stories high and surrounded by large trees and beautiful gardens. The lawns lead down to a creek at the bottom of the garden where ducks frolicked and many lovely Australian birds enjoyed the native bushes and gum trees.

Rupert Penfield was a wealthy man, mainly through inheritances, and more recently through discovery of gold on his land. He had many gold leases. He was a chubby man, short of stature, with a short beard, his nature reasonable and calm. He adored his wife, Priscilla, whom he met and fell in love with when they were both eighteen, At that time Priscilla was "coming out" in English Society and was considered to be quiet a beauty. Nowadays she was trying to cover her once reddish hair with various potions to cover increasing grey, and mixing other cosmetic creams to avoid ageing. She was very vain and terrified of getting old. Priscilla hated Australia, considering it to be a rough country, lacking in sophistication and without any real substance. She complained constantly to Rupert, "Rupert, I just hate this awful place, why can't we go home to England?"

Rupert's answer was to buy her some beautiful lingerie or new jewels to try to keep her happy which worked for a while until she became bored again.

Charlotte

The Penfields had a daughter named Charlotte, who came with them to Australia when she was just seven years old. Charlotte hated Australia with a vengeance since the day she stepped onto the dock in Melbourne as a young child. Charlotte was a most unpleasant girl with a nasty, unfriendly nature. She hated everyone and everything. Nothing could ever make Charlotte happy. As a baby she was restless. She refused to eat and threw her food at her nanny. She did not walk until she was three, not because she couldn't but because she was lazy. The Penfields employed two nannies to look after the unpleasant disobedient girl who was given everthing a girl could ever want. "I hate this awful place, I want to go home to England," she would scream at her father on a regular basis. He would say to his wife, "I don't know what we did to have such a mean nasty girl."

Now ten years later, Charlotte was seventeen and the Penfields were desperate to find a husband for their wilful daughter. Charlotte was a pretty girl but it was hard to tell what she looked like as she painted her face with garish coloured cosmetics which made her look like a clown. Charlotte thought she looked beautiful but since she always had a mean nasty frown on her face and with the horrible make up she certainly was no beauty. She hated to bathe so her golden hair always looked greasy and unattractive.

The Penfields had tried to educate Charlotte by employing the best tutors, all of whom left due to her rudeness or other such poor behaviour. The music teacher left when she threw a vase of flowers at him, smashing the glass and cutting him badly on the chin. She did not even apologise. Her English teacher left after Charlotte threw a chair out of the window and narrowly missed hitting her in the head. Consequently Charlotte remained poorly educated. She had no skills in English or maths, and could barely read, preferring to read penny dreadfuls with pictures or comic books.

Charlotte had been engaged three times to very eligible men in the new colony. The first was Daniel Moore, a wealthy sheep farmer with an inheritance. Charlotte was rude to him when left alone, calling him "big ears". He lasted just three weeks. Then there was Andrew McDonald, son of the vicar, who also had an inheritance. He tried to have a conversation with Charlotte and left after discovering that she could barely read nor write. Number three was a lovely quiet man called John Werribee who was a wealthy landowner. When introduced to his mother after getting engaged, Charlotte said her mother in law to be, looked like a cross between a monkey and a pig, which John felt to be highly insulting and immediately called off the engagement. Now the Penfields were again holding parties and soirees in an attempt to find a husband for Charlotte. Charlotte's response to it all was "I don't want to get married, I hate men, they are horrible creatures."

In spite of her feelings Rupert and Priscilla were determined to find a husband for Charlotte, even if they had to buy one for her. The years of coping with her had taken their toll and both of them wanted a more peaceful life.

In the kitchen area of the big house known as "Seven Oaks", life continued in much the same vein as it had for many years. The servants saw very little of the owners or their wilful daughter, but screams and shouts were heard daily as Charlotte's parents tried to deal with her. One governess after another departed the house, as Charlotte was either rude to them or abused and bullied them. They had now resorted to bringing in a governess from Melbourne and pay double the wages in order to keep her.

Molly had found an old mirror in one of the sheds and could see her beautiful figure and lovely golden locks and blue eyes. She still wore her fake spectacles and wore her hair in its usual tight bun. Molly now had one afternoon a week off and was receiving a small wage which she saved for a rainy day. On her day off she went for a long walk near the creek, admiring the beautiful native plants and animals. As she walked home one day, Mrs Banks and Mrs Beale were watching her running across the grass with a bunch of wildflowers in her hand, her hair billowing around her shoulders. Mrs Banks said, "That girl reminds me of someone, I can't think who." To which Mrs Beale replied, "I know what you mean, I see a likeness to someone as well."

A new suitor appeared on the scene. His name was Richard Darley and he was a wealthy landowner who had received inheritances from his grandmother and an aunt in England as well as finding gold on some of his many gold leases. Richard was a very handsome man, tall with light blonde hair and blue eyes. He was considered a most eligible bachelor in the new land, with many mothers trying to snare him as a husband for their young daughters. The Penfields organised several parties and dinners, always making sure that Charlotte spent only a short time with him.

Eventually after some months, he asked Charlotte if she wished to marry him, but firstly asked her if she wanted children. "Do you like children Charlotte?" Richard asked. She replied, "Of course I do Richard, I just love the little dears." Richard told her he was very keen to start a family as soon as possible and was pleased with her answer. The Penfields were over the moon to think that such a man had proposed to Charlotte and suggested that the marriage take place as soon as possible. They agreed on a church wedding with the reception at "Seven Oaks" in a month's time.

The servants were called to a meeting after Mrs Banks and Mrs Beale were informed of the intended wedding of Miss Charlotte. The Penfields were keen to have the marriage take place as soon as possible, knowing that Charlotte could become a problem if they waited and the groom had no objections, wanting to start a family as soon as possible, so the wedding would take place in just four weeks' time. It was to be held in the newly built stone church in Ballarat, followed by a luncheon at "Seven Oaks", catered for by Mrs Banks and her team.

Mrs Banks called Molly into the kitchen to tell her the news. "Miss Charlotte has got engaged and we are to do the wedding reception so I will need your help very much in the next few weeks" she said. "Oh how exciting'" replied Molly. "To be honest dear I am a little nervous about it all," said Mrs Banks. "I am sure you will do a wonderful job Mrs Banks, since you are known all around town to be the very best cook," said Molly sincerely. "Thank you my dear, I feel more confident now," replied Mrs Banks, as they set off to the kitchen to meet with Mrs Beale to sit down and work out a plan of action.

Work started immediately in preparation for the big event to take place in just four weeks, not giving them much time to do it all. Mrs Banks started to soak the fruit to make the wedding cake and Molly watched with excitement. The gardeners worked overtime to ensure that the grounds looked perfect. All of the best china had to be washed and dried and glass ware and silver polished. Molly found herself run off her feet and sinking into bed exhausted each night. In spite of feeling tired she enjoyed all of the wedding preparations and willingly completed all of the tasks given to her. After two weeks Mrs Banks gave Molly a full day off as a reward for her hard work. Molly decided to take a packed lunch and to take a long walk along the riverbank.

4

The Storm

Molly left "Seven Oaks" on a sunny morning with her golden curls flowing over her shoulders, leaving her apron and spectacles behind. She took the walking track along the river most used by visitors and locals alike. She stopped to eat her lunch, noticing that the sun was slipping behind the clouds which were gathering in different shades of grey in the sky. She walked on, until it started to rain, just slightly at first and then heavily, making visibility difficult. She came upon an old shed at the bottom of someone's garden and rushed quickly to it, entering through the half open door and sitting on a bail of hay.

Soon after, the door opened further and a man with a horse emerged, also taking shelter from the storm. "My dear, what are you doing here, dripping wet?" he asked. Molly replied, "I was out walking and became caught in the storm," said Molly as she gazed at the tall figure of the beautiful blue eyed, golden haired man standing before her. "Come sit with me here and I will warm you up," said the tall *stranger*. Molly did as he asked, quite mesmerized by his gentleness and charm. Soon he had his arms around her and was kissing her deeply. Molly had never been held in such a manner or kissed before so she was excited at the beautiful feelings surging through her body. She was not frightened or in any way dismayed at what was happening. Rather she felt complete trust in the man as if she had known him all of her life. The stranger continued fondling her breasts and then undressed her and himself. They made love at first gently and then more deeply as the storm raged outside the barn. Molly could hardly believe the wondrous feeling she was experiencing. Finally, she realized darkness was approaching outside and quickly dressed herself. "I must go, I will be late," she said to the lovely man. "I hope I did not hurt you dearest," he said as Molly started for the door. "No it was wonderful, thank you," replied Molly as she ran out of the barn door. As they left to go in different directions, they looked to the sky to see a double rainbow appear.

Molly ran home as fast as she could and quickly tied her hair into the usual bun and placed the spectacles on her nose, reporting to Mrs Banks, full of apologies for being late. "Don't worry, my dear, you deserve some time away from here," said Mrs Banks with a smile.

Riding back to his home, Richard wondered why his bride to be needed to rush away so quickly. She was absolutely delightful and he could hardly wait to make her his wife and to have children with her.

After doing her evening chores, Molly retired to her comfortable bed, where for the first time she could try to make sense of what had happened that very afternoon. Molly had almost no knowledge of how adults expressed their love for each other but she assumed that what happened to her and the handsome man today might qualify as an expression of love. It seemed strange to her that the man seemed to know her, but she had never seen him before in her life.

A Wedding

The four weeks until the big event went quickly by as the servants and Mrs Banks along with Molly worked each day preparing delicious food for the one hundred guests who would enjoy the morning wedding of Miss Charlotte. Priscilla and Rupert managed to keep Richard away from meeting with Charlotte in case she misbehaved and the wedding would be called off.

A beautiful wedding dress was made for Charlotte, who when trying it on for her last fitting, threatened to cut it into a hundred pieces. "I hate this dress, I just hate it, I am going to tear it up," she screamed, as her mother and the dressmaker hurriedly removed the dress. Priscilla then took the dress and locked it up in a cupboard with a padlock. Three little girls, distant cousins were bribed to be bridesmaids, wearing lovely pale blue gowns with tiny posies of mixed flowers. Charlotte became more and more difficult to manage as the wedding day drew closer and Priscilla called the doctor to obtain a medicine to calm her down. The medicine was put into her morning cup of tea and things were more pleasant until the medicine wore off each day and then the yelling and screaming would start again.

At last the big day arrived and the house looked beautiful with large vases of flowers everywhere. Mrs Banks had made different types of savouries, and a light luncheon was to take place following the service in the newly built Anglican Church. Priscilla gave Charlotte a double dose of the medicine so she was quiet dopey when her dressmaker dressed her. The gown was beautiful but Charlotte still insisted on plastering her face with the horrid make-up and with the scowl permanently fixed on her face, Charlotte could hardly be described as a beautiful bride.

Charlotte departed for the church with her father in one carriage and Priscilla went in another carriage with the three little girls, all hoping that they could stay as far away from Charlotte as possible. After about an hour, the family arrived home with Charlotte now a married woman at last. The food was served to the many well dressed guests, and corks popped as sparkling wine was served to all. Guests all sent compliments to the cook, making Mrs Banks beam with pleasure. Finally all the guests left, the married couple left in a coach for their honeymoon and Rupert and Priscilla headed to their room, elated that they had finally got Charlotte married. "I can hardly believe it Rupert, she is finally gone," said Priscilla. "I know my dear, I feel like a free man at last," replied Rupert with a grin from ear to ear.

Mrs Banks, Mrs Beale and Molly finally sat down after all of the kitchen was cleaned up and sampled some of the leftovers including the sparkling wine. "Oh, this is so wonderful, I have never tasted wine before," said Molly, munching away on some of the beautiful savouries as she drank her wine.

6

The Honeymoon

Richard and Charlotte set off in the coach for Melbourne where they were booked into one of the new hotels popping up in Melbourne as the city grew. Richard looked forward to his wedding night, but was surprised that his new wife was so silent. She had on such a lot of make-up as well and Richard knew that her skin was beautiful and soft. She did not need make-up. Her maid sat silently as well. Richard did not want the maid to come but Charlotte insisted, so he gave in.

They arrived at the hotel and Charlotte waltzed inside where they were warmly greeted by the staff. She ignored them all and demanded to be taken to her room immediately. Richard was embarrassed at her rudeness, but followed her upstairs to their suite. Charlotte was already ordering her maid around as Richard invited her to join him for dinner in the dining room. She told him she did not wish to eat and he insisted "It is our wedding day Charlotte, and I expect you to join me at dinner," said Richard firmly. Charlotte got up and with a sour look on her face followed Richard to the dining room. The chef had prepared a beautiful meal for them, but Charlotte just picked at her food saying, "I hate this food, I wish to go to my room now." Richard was furious. He stayed and enjoyed his lovely meal and made an excuse to the chef that Charlotte was feeling unwell. He then went for a long walk in the city before returning to his room and to Charlotte.

When he entered their suite Charlotte was already in bed. He climbed in beside her and she screamed loudly. "What are you doing in my bed, get out now," yelled Charlotte in a frenzy. Richard, already cross with Charlotte replied,"This is my bed as well Charlotte. We are married now and I wish to start a family as soon as possible, now take off your nightgown or I will take it off for you." For a moment Charlotte was going to disobey him, but she changed her mind at the tone of his voice and the look of fury on his face. Richard then took her in his arms and made love to her while she remained unresponsive and angry. When it was over she moved as far away as she could from him in the large bed, silently cursing him and hating him.

Richard was stunned. He could not believe that the woman he just married was the same woman that he held in his arms just a few days ago, who willingly gave herself to him in a loving caring way. What had happened to make Charlotte change in such a short time to become an unpleasant nasty shrew. The next day Richard woke up to find out that Charlotte and her maid had gone to the large department stores to shop. In a way he was glad. He went to the dining room and ate a tasteful leisurely breakfast, followed by a nice long walk admiring the new city buildings. There was no sign of Charlotte that day until she arrived home loaded with parcels from various stores, demanding at the top of her voice for staff to take her purchases to her room. She did not speak to Richard when they met in the hall. The following day was similar to the first and by the fourth day Richard had reached breaking point and decided to put his foot down. "Be ready at eight am in the morning, we will be going home," Richard told Charlotte. "But I have not yet finished my shopping," moaned Charlotte. "In case you have forgotten Charlotte, we are supposed to be on our honeymoon, not a shopping spree. I have hardly seen you and you will not share my bed, so we may as well be home where I can get some work done," said Richard in an angry tone. It took a lot to anger him, but he was fed up with Charlotte and her ways and they had only been married a few days.

Charlotte screamed and yelled at Richard, cursing him and saying, "I hate you, I hate you, you are a mean beast." Richard responded by telling her to get her bags packed immediately ready for the morning. The following morning Charlotte dragged herself to the coach with her poor maid worn out already, carrying a huge load of boxes. Richard felt sorry for the maid but did not interfere, not wanting to assist Charlotte in any way.

The coach ride home was completed in silence. Richard read several newspapers whilst the maid slept and Charlotte sat in a corner sulking and pouting. Richard was extremely glad to see the coach pull into Ballarat. He was even more glad to return to his beautiful home "Darley Park".

His home was magnificent. Built with convict labour, it closely resembled his ancestral home back in England. Mainly built of stone with wide verandahs and glorious grounds which were a mixture of native and English shrubs and trees, Richard loved his charming rambling country estate. Charlotte flew out of the coach with her poor maid following and started yelling at the servants who were all lined up to welcome their master's new bride. She ignored their good wishes leaving Richard to apologise, telling them that Charlotte and had a nervous disposition. He was happy to be home and assured his staff of that fact, hoping that he would not lose any of his servants because of Charlotte. He immediately gave them all a pay increase and arranged for a second maid for Charlotte.

Richard made his way to the library and locked the door. He could hear Charlotte barking orders at the servants and yelling and screaming, which became the norm at "Darley Park" over the next few weeks. Richard was at a loss as to know what to do about Charlotte. He decided to visit "Seven Oaks" to speak to her parents. Priscilla and Rupert were friendly but not forthcoming with any information about their daughter. "She has a nervous nature," said

Priscilla "And she gets a little bit upset at times," said Rupert. Richard left then, knowing full well that they were lying. He now understood why the Penfield's were in such a hurry to have the wedding in just four weeks.

A few weeks after the wedding, Charlotte became more aggressive and nasty than usual and servants came to Richard wanting to leave. He persuaded them to stay with a higher wage and assurances that he would get a doctor for Charlotte. He contacted Dr Brown who had seen her before. Dr Brown explained to Richard that he felt Charlotte was suffering from an illness of a mental kind which her parents had refused to treat but now would require medicine daily to calm her down. He asked to examine Charlotte who was not too happy to be touched by a man even with her maid present. Charlotte resisted the Doctor's request to examine her, but Richard physically picked her up and took her to the Library, screaming and kicking, where she was to meet with the Doctor. Following his examination, Dr Brown asked to see Richard in the Library. Richard made his way there, wondering what problem he would now have to face with his difficult unpleasant wife.

Dr Brown said, "Richard, are you aware that your wife is pregnant, about three months I would say. That would explain her recent aggressive behaviour." Richard was stunned for a moment until reality set in and he replied, "Pregnant, you say, that is what I have always wanted. It must have happened on our wedding night because that is the only time Charlotte has let me anywhere near her." The doctor went on to say that there would be every possibility that Charlotte would try to abort the baby and that she would need to be carefully watched at all times to prevent such a thing occurring. Dr Brown left then, leaving Richard with the task of telling Charlotte of the pregnancy.

Richard then told Charlotte of the pregnancy, and the anticipated eruption and temper tantrum followed, ending with Charlotte storming out of the library and demanding a carriage to be brought to her immediately. Richard caught her and locked her in her room un til he could inform the servants about what Charlotte might try to do. From then on, Charlotte was watched night and day, guarded by Richard's loyal servants.

The pregnancy was a difficult one, with morning sickness and Charlotte's refusal to eat making things much worse than they needed to be. The doctor told Richard not to worry too much, as babies were tough little things and Charlotte was strong and healthy. She was a dreadful patient, moaning and groaning about her predicament, shouting at her maids and abusing other servants. She made several attempts to go to an abortionist, but each time was stopped by a groom or another servant. Richard found the whole process very tiring and upsetting and spent as little time at his beautiful home as possible. He took up offices in Ballarat city and spent his time there during the day, only returning in the evening to ride his horse and have dinner.

Richard started to make plans for the baby as the months flew by. He obtained the services of an experienced midwife and explained to her his wife's mental condition, offering to pay double the going rate for deliveries. "Don't worry young man, this old girl has seen it all, I will be the boss when the pains start coming," she laughed. Richard started to purchase clothes and nappies for the coming baby. When he returned one evening he found that Charlotte had ripped them into shreds. He purchased more clothes and put them in a locked cupboard, but not before giving Charlotte a telling off. "You may not want this baby, but I do and if you ever do anything like that again, I will remove your maids permanently," he said shaking with anger, yet trying to hide it. As punishment he gave Charlotte's maids two days off. He returned to the shops and purchased more baby clothes and a crib and baby carriage which he hid in one of the sheds, knowing full well that Charlotte would never look for anything in a shed.

The weeks turned to months and Charlotte became huge which put her in an even worse temper. "Get this thing out of me," she screamed each day. Richard was pleased to see the baby grow. He could hardly wait to meet his son or daughter. Richard went to the employment service to find a nanny for his baby. He knew that Charlotte would have nothing to do with the child so he needed to find a nanny who could start work immediately the child came into the world. There were a number of nannies to choose from but he ended up choosing a woman called Grace Jones. She had been married and had lost her husband and child with whooping cough a year ago, now finding it hard to make ends meet. Grace was happy to move to "Darley Park" immediately in preparation for the arrival of Richard's heir.

Shortly after Richard hired the nanny, Charlotte went into labour one morning and of course she made such a fuss, everyone in the household knew about it. Richard sent for the midwife who told him that Charlotte was only in the early stage of labour and it would probably be a long labour because she was so unco-operative. Richard took off for the day, unwilling to listen to Charlotte's screams and cries for help. "Please help me, I am dying," she repeated as the labour progressed. The midwife tried to get her to relax and breathe slowly, but Charlotte did not realise that she herself was making the labour longer with her aggressive behaviour. The doctor was called and said labour was progressing well if a little slow due to her constant tantrums. He ordered a potion to calm her down, but said the birth would be a few hours away.

Finally after being in labour all day and well into the night, Charlotte gave birth to twins, a boy and a girl at two am in the morning. Richard gazed at the two perfect babies and fell in love with them at first sight. The twins weighed about five pounds each and were very healthy. Charlotte did not even want to see them. "Get them away from me," she screamed when the midwife handed them to her. "I hate the horrible things that have given me so much terrible pain," she yelled. The twins were taken into the nursery immediately and the nanny took control of their care, preparing bottles of milk. Richard visited them straight away, cuddling them in the big rocking chair in the nursery. He decided to name them Samuel James and Emily Anne after his grandparents.

Little Samuel and Emily looked very much like their father with his lovely deep blue eyes and fair hair. Their skin was soft and golden and their father adored them, talking softly to them and rubbing his large hands across their tiny backs.

As the days went on, Richard spent as much time as he could with his twins, watching them grow, smile, sit up and then start to crawl. He never saw his wife who slept for three days after the birth, giving the servants a much needed break As soon as she was up and about again she turned her interest to the latest fashions in Paris and experimenting with make-up even more hideous than usual. She never saw the twins or asked about them.

Richard decided to have the twins baptised in the same church in which he had married Charlotte. The minister remembered him and the service was arranged for the following Saturday. All of his servants were invited and a few neighbours and friends. He organised with his cook to have a small reception with savouries and sparkling wine after the church service. Nanny Grace was sent to a large department store to purchase two Christening outfits for the twins, who at six months looked quiet delightful. Their hair had grown now into golden curls and with their bonnets they were a picture to behold. Richard rode to his in-laws, the Penfields, to invite them to the Christening, but they refused, saying they had another engagement which Richard did not believe. They had never seen the twins, nor shown any interest in getting to know their only grandchildren. That fact Richard found difficult to understand. He knew that his parents and sister in England were very excited and could hardly wait to meet their grandchildren. In fact they were planning a trip to Australia sometimes in the next few months.

The christening when off without any problems. Richard tried his level best to get Charlotte to attend, but she flatly refused saying,"No way am I going anywhere with those horrible little brats." Richard was disappointed for his children but glad in a way that she would not be around to have a tantrum or create a scene in front of their guests. A lovely morning tea was held after the church service and then tired out, they were put down for their nap, even though their father was reluctant to let them out of his sight when they looked so beautiful.

Richard was so proud of his children and thought the nanny was doing a splendid job. He did however notice that she had begun to flirt a little with him and try to draw his attention to herself more than he would like. He took no notice of her actions and always treated her in a professional manner, making his conversations at all times with her about his son and daughter. Grace would try to make their conversations more personal but Richard would have none of it.

Charlotte was becoming bored and restless and Richard was worried that she might harm the children. He made sure that nanny Grace was always accompanied by another servant when they left the house for their daily walks in their pushchairs and when inside a servant always stood on watch. Charlotte was permitted to leave the house but only accompanied by a servant and her maid. Richard had no idea where she went, and he simply did not care.

Otherwise they were a lovely happy family, just without a loving mother. Richard made sure that the children's rooms and his own were at the opposite end of the house to Charlotte's so that they did not hear the daily abuse and aggressive behaviour of their mother.

PART
Two

Ben

After Molly had been at "Seven Oaks" for five years, and due to her continuous excellent work ethic, Mrs Banks made a suggestion to Mrs Beale "Do you think we could get Molly's sentence reduced. I believe she only stole a small packet of oats to feed her sick father," she said. Mrs Beale agreed "I think that is a wonderful idea Mrs Banks," replied Mrs Beale. And so it was that the two ladies started the ball rolling to get Molly's sentenced reduced.

Molly would always be grateful to Mrs Banks and Mrs Beale for suggesting that she get a reduction of her sentence from seven to five years. The Penfields reluctantly agreed, not really interested in what the servants did, so after serving just five years Molly finally regained her freedom and was granted her ticket of leave. It was with mixed feelings that Molly considered her future as a free woman. She was now twenty two years old and a beautiful young woman, but her knowledge of the outside world was very limited.

Molly left the only place she called home as a convict, farewelled by the two ladies who had guided her and advised her over the first few difficult months and then years. She had learned so much from them. Mrs Beale found two dresses which her daughter in law no longer wanted which fitted Molly perfectly and some shoes and bonnets, so Molly set off to the employment office looking very respectable. It was a tearful goodbye for all three as Molly left through the front foyer of the house to walk to the town and the next stage of her life. She still remembered her entrance through the back door five years ago as a seventeen year old convict. Molly made her way straight to the office with her two references tucked in her hold all. On presenting them to the officer he said "I know of Mrs Banks and her cooking skills, if you have worked with her I am sure you have been well taught. There is a man currently looking for a cook for his boarding house. Do you think you could manage to do that?" he asked. Molly replied, "I'm sure that I can try, I have just helped cook for a big wedding at my last place of work and it was not at all difficult." "Well then, the owner is Mr Ben Chandler and here is the address," he replied. Molly made her way to the address and found a beautifully presented large two storey white timber building with a small neat garden out the front and geraniums hanging from pots from window sills. Molly had a good feeling about the place as she knocked on the front door and entered what was to become her new home and place of work.

Ben Chandler, the owner opened the door and invited Molly into his library, asking a servant to bring a pot of tea. Ben was a man in his late forties, nice looking with light brown hair and blue eyes with a short beard. He asked Molly lots of questions including whether she felt that she could manage a large group of guests, to which Molly replied, "I can only but try Mr Chandler." Ben was happy with her answer and they agreed on a three months trial. Ben then asked one of the servants to show Molly to her room which was on the second floor. It was a lovely room, larger than the one at "Seven Oaks". It contained a big bed with a lace coverlet and soft down pillows, There was a window overlooking a lake and a cupboard for her clothes as well as a wash-stand and a wool rug on the floor. Molly was quiet enchanted with the room. "Oh how lovely this room is," she exclaimed to the servant who told her that Ben's late wife had designed and furnished every room in the boarding house before she died.

Molly put on her new uniform with a large pinny in pale blue and started work straight away baking bread and making pies for desserts. She made boiled mutton with white sauce and fresh vegetables followed by bread and butter pudding with cream. The meal was a success and Molly's first day ended well. Ben invited Molly into his library for coffee after dinner and the clean up. She sat down on the chair he offered and he told her about his wife and how much he had loved her. "It was our dream to one day own a boarding house. We were both teachers back in England and came to Australia to start a different life. After we arrived and built the boarding house she was so happy. Her name was Eloise and she was French," Ben said sadly unable to control his tears. Molly talked gently to him about his wife, letting him express his sorrow which had been building up inside him for the past three months, since Eloise passed away.

The next few weeks were very busy at the boarding house as news spread about Molly's cooking skills. Ben took her shopping each week for groceries and fresh meat and vegetables. He insisted in her using only the best ingredients in her cooking. Molly asked him if she could start a vegetable garden and run some chooks for fresh eggs. Naturally he agreed and before long the chooks were laying and Molly had fresh eggs for her breakfasts and custards. Molly and Ben had coffee each evening and Ben read poetry to her and taught her to read. She had learnt some reading her father and Ben offered her a higher level of language which she greatly appreciated.

After Molly had been at the boarding house for three months, one day she felt a little unwell as if she was in for a dose of flu which was going around. Ben insisted that she go to see the doctor. "I have never been to a doctor Ben, I am sure it will pass," said Molly, but Ben insisted, saying that they could now afford for her to see a doctor. Ben he took her in his buggy to see his own doctor, Dr Brown. Molly was taken into a room and asked to put on a gown by a nurse. She felt very nervous at her first doctor's visit. The nurse said, "don't be worried dear, Dr Brown is a kind, gentle man and he will look after you." Molly immediately felt better and soon the nurse took her into the doctor's room. Dr Brown stood up and said, "Welcome Molly, I understand you are a little bit nervous, but I assure you I will not hurt you." He asked Molly to hop onto the bed so he could examine her to find out what was making her unwell. Following the examination, He asked her to put on her own clothes and go into his other office for a talk.

Molly sat on the chair opposite Dr Brown waiting for him to speak. "Do you know what is wrong with me?" asked Molly nervously. "Yes my dear, I do. You are pregnant. You can expect to have a little baby boy or girl in about six months time," he said. "Pregnant, are you sure Dr Brown," said Molly, shocked to the core. "How can I be pregnant, I am not married," she stuttered. "Have you made love with a man about three months ago?" Dr Brown asked. "Well yes, there was one time when I was caught in a storm and a stranger sheltered with me in a barn," replied Molly. "Is that when my baby was made," she asked. "Yes, most likely. Molly you do know about where babies come from don't you?" asked Dr Brown. Molly replied, "Well no, I did not know, I suppose I never really thought about it. I don't know what I shall do now. I am unmarried and pregnant and an ex convict as well so no-one will ever want me." Dr Brown advised her to talk to Ben about it and to go home and get some rest.

8

Molly's Joy

Molly went home in the buggy with Ben and told him she would discuss her visit to the doctor with him after dinner that night. She started dinner preparations in a daze, still stunned by the news that she would become a mother in a few months time. There were only a few guests for dinner that night much to Molly's relief. After dinner, she and Ben retired to the library where she told Ben everything that Dr Brown had told her. "I feel so ashamed Ben, especially since I have no husband, said Molly sadly. "Do you love this man Molly?" asked Ben. "I hardly know him Ben, I just met him once when we took shelter in a barn during a storm. I do know that I felt strong feelings for him. I had no idea that what we did would result in a baby. I never thought about where babies came from. I have led a very sheltered life. I expect my mother would have told me, but since I became a convict at sixteen and then working in the one place for five years I have no knowledge of worldly things," said Molly seriously. Ben suggested that Molly go to bed and get some rest and that they would talk some more in the morning. "Try not to worry my dear, we will work something out I am sure," said Ben kindly. Molly walked slowly up the stairs to her room where she lay awake trying to work out what she would do. Eventually to she fell asleep out of sheer exhaustion.

Morning came and with it, the realisation for Molly that she was going to have a baby. She touched her still flat tummy, hardly believing that her body housed a little baby. She went downstairs to start breakfast, to find that Ben was in the kitchen wooding up the stove and boiling the kettle. She started to make the porridge, giving Ben a shy smile and then moved on to bacon and eggs, serving guests and then servants. Ben organised the toast and tea and coffee. Following breakfast when the servants were busy making beds, Ben took Molly into the library for a talk.

"I have been thinking about your situation, Molly and I might have a solution if you are willing. Firstly this is a suggestion only and you do not have to feel in any way obliged to accept. Would you consider marrying me to give your baby a name and to make you a respectable married woman in the eyes of the community. I do not mind if you would rather bring up your child alone. You will still have your job here. I have only had one love in my life and that was Eloise, so it will be a convenient marriage only and I will not expect you to share my bed. What do you say?" Molly stood up and hugged Ben saying, "Oh Ben, you are such an amazing man, of course I will marry you. It will be a great honour. You are such a kind and generous man, thank you from the bottom of my heart."

Ben and Molly told the servants that they were to be married in a week's time. They then made arrangements with the magistrate at the court house and Ben took Molly to the largest department store in town to purchase a suitable outfit in which she could be married. "You can hardly be married in your pinny," laughed Ben. Molly and Ben chose a pale pink outfit with matching bonnet and shoes.

The marriage took place at the court house a week later. Ben looked smart in his suit and Molly was beautiful in her new outfit. Her golden curls peeped out from under her bonnet. Ben handed her a posy of pale pink roses as they walked into the magistrate's office. With the official service over, Ben and Molly made their way home to where the servants had set out savouries prepared by Molly, fruit cake and sparkling wine to celebrate. Servants and guests staying at the boarding house joined in to congratulate the newly married couple. Molly looked happy, as did Ben, both sure that they had done the right thing. After the celebration, Ben insisted that Molly have a rest until tea time, She agreed, feeling a bit tired after all of the excitement of the day.

Life for Ben and Molly Chandler continued in a calm and pleasant way, just as it had before their marriage. Molly continued to do all of the cooking and Ben organised extra help for her, so she now had an assistant called Jenny who proved to be a wonderful asset to Molly. People kept coming to the boarding house in droves and Ben was delighted with its success. He worried about Molly overdoing things and insisted on her having a daytime nap "Molly, you are carrying our baby and I know you are fit and healthy, but I want you to stay that way," said Ben.

Molly managed to keep her pregnancy quiet for some time as her large pinny hid her now large baby bump. As the months passed, she and Ben still had coffee after dinner. Molly had been taught to knit by one of the older servants and was busy knitting tiny baby clothes. Ben made a cradle out of wood and they purchased a baby carriage. Ben and Molly found a suitable midwife recommended by one of the servants. She was a motherly soul named Alice, a very experienced midwife, having delivered many babies over the years. Molly felt comfortable with her after they chatted. It was agreed that the midwife would be collected by Ben when the first signs of labour started since Molly was a first time inexperienced mother to be.

A few days before her expected due date Molly who by then looked like a beached whale, went into labour when her water broke. Ben hastened to the midwife's house and brought Alice back to the boarding house where she immediately took charge, trying to get Molly to relax as her labour progressed. After a few hours of hard labour for Molly and anxiety for Ben waiting outside her room, soon a baby's cry could be heard, then another cry shortly after. Molly gave birth to twins, a boy and a girl. Alice took the babies out to Ben who fell in love with them instantly. Molly was very excited to have given birth to twins, "They are so beautiful Ben don't you think?" she said with a huge smile. "Absolutely, the most beautiful babies in the world," replied Ben as he placed his finger in the hand of the little boy.

Ben wanted to name the little boy Richard Benjamin after his father and Molly chose the name Sarah Emily after her mother for the little girl. The babies both weighed over six pounds and Molly started breast feeding immediately, fortunate to have plenty of milk for two babies. After two weeks, Molly insisted on going back into the kitchen, in spite of Ben's opposition. She fitted in her feeds with meal preparation and relied heavily on Jenny in the first few weeks. Gradually the babies started to sleep through the night and Molly regained her strength. Ben adored his children from the word go and spent hours with them. It didn't matter that he was not their biological father, in every way he was the most loving caring father any child could have.

Molly and Ben between them managed to give their two little children all the love and care they could manage, as well as keep their boarding house running smoothly. It was now a very profitable concern, but both Molly and Ben thought of it as a labour of love. They enjoyed meeting different people from everywhere and of course the twins were enjoyed by all of their guests both young and old. Molly enjoyed taking the twins for their walk in their double baby carriage each afternoon after they had a nap and they usually took the same route along the river. The twins enjoyed seeing the kangaroos and koalas, and the pretty wild flowers along the way as much as Molly had when she took her walks from "Seven Oaks" as a convict. The twins were now nine months old and could sit up and were just crawling, following Molly everywhere in the kitchen. It was at those times that Ben took over, relieving Molly so she could do her work. Both children resembled Molly with blue eyes and golden curls. They had a placid nature, rarely crying and were usually happy cheerful children.

A Shock

One calm sunny day Molly set off as usual for her walk, taking her usual route, with the twins gurgling away in their own baby language. As she approached a bend in the river she thought she saw what looked like an animal, lying face down in the water amongst the reeds. She left the twins in their pushchair and went over to take a closer look. Molly called out in shock, "Oh no, it cannot be." She could hardly believe what she was seeing. It was a young woman, not an animal and the oddest thing was that the woman was so like herself. It was like looking at herself in the mirror. The woman looked about her age and was deathly white and not breathing. Molly assumed that she had had drowned in the murky water and caught in the reeds. Her clothes were expensive but covered in mud and reeds. Molly looked around and saw two small shapes, also in the water. She went across to the shapes and saw two small bodies face down. When she turned them over she saw two small babies, almost identical to her own twins, also dead. Molly was devastated. She did not know what to do at first, still in shock. When she stopped shaking she took the twins and ran to the road where she asked a couple out walking their dog to go and get the police and ambulance. "Quick, go quickly," Molly screamed. The couple took off and Molly went back to the horrible scene where three dead bodies lay. "Who were those people, why had they died and why did the woman look so much like her and the children so much like her own twins if slightly smaller?" Molly asked herself, her mind filled with questions with no answers coming.

Shortly after, but for Molly what seemed like hours, the police arrived and were followed closely by the ambulance. The policeman in charge questioned Molly at length. One of the policemen thought he recognised the woman as Mrs Darley, wife of Mr Richard Darley. A policeman was sent to the home of Mr Richard Darley who arrived at the scene a short time later. Molly stood in the background among the tall gum trees watching the drama unfolding before her eyes. She saw a tall handsome man arrive on his horse and fall to his knees sobbing uncontrollably as he took his two babies in his arms. Molly recognised him as the man she made love with on the night of the storm, the father of her twins. Not able to watch anymore and with the twins becoming restless, Molly turned and walked sadly and slowly home.

After dinner when Molly and Ben had their coffee together Molly told Ben how she had found the woman and her two babies drowned in the river. She did not tell him about the likeness to herself and her twins, nor the fact that she saw the father of her twins, thinking that he did not need to know those details because they might upset him. "Do you think it was murder or suicide?" asked Ben. "I think the mother drowned the children first and then herself," replied Molly sadly. "What a terrible thing to happen, I feel so sorry for the poor father," said Ben. Yes, he must be really suffering," replied Molly, thinking of the way the father knelt down and sobbed over his dead babies.

Tragedy

R ichard needed to take a trip to Melbourne for the day to attend to business. He advised all of his servants and Nanny Grace that Charlotte had been particularly nasty and unsettled over the past few days and they were to watch her very closely in case she attempted to harm the twins or leave the estate. The twins were growing up fast now and at nine months were delightful. Sammy and his sister Emily were a source of great joy for Richard who spent hours with them, reading to them in the evenings and taking them for walks in their baby carriages every day. He was planning to take them to meet his parents and his sister in England once they were a little bit older, knowing that his family would love them as much as he did. Charlotte took no interest in the children's welfare, ignoring them completely. Richard could not understand how a mother could not love such beautiful children. They were happy babies, sitting up and getting ready to crawl, now starting to talk. Richard was thrilled when Emily said dada for the first time.

He left on the coach in the early morning, hoping to be back for story time with the children later in the day. When he arrived home he found that Charlotte and the babies were missing. All servants and nanny Grace were searching the entire estate, including sheds and barns and the police had been notified. Richard was beside himself. He started to have a very bad feeling about it all. Nanny Grace was questioned at length. It appeared that she had fallen asleep in a chair beside the cribs of the twins who were asleep for their afternoon nap. When she woke the twins were gone. She had never fallen asleep before and when she woke she felt that she had been drugged.

When the policeman came to the door to get Richard, he immediately got on his horse and went to the area described by the policeman. When he arrived he could hardly believe what he saw. His beautiful babies whom he loved more than anything else in the world were lying lifeless in the shallow water, not breathing, pale and still. He sank to his knees and took them into his arms, sobbing uncontrollably. "No, no, it can't be true, it must be a bad dream," he sobbed. "Get some blankets to warm them up?" he asked the policeman. Soon after, the policeman went to Richard and persuaded him to release the children. Reluctantly he did, even though he never wanted to let them go. He glanced at his dead wife and cursed her "Why did you do this, why kill innocent children, you are a wicked evil woman," he screamed at the top of his voice. He told the police not to take the woman with the children in the undertaker's cart, but to separate them. "I do not want her anywhere near my babies," said Richard shaking from head to toe with grief and anger.

Richard went home and told his servants what had happened. He asked nanny Grace to get the twins' christening clothes out and took them to the undertaker's himself. He held his little dead babies for hours until the undertaker forced him to leave them. Richard returned home a broken man to his house devoid of the happy laughter of his two adorable children. The next day after no sleep Richard called nanny Grace into his library and dismissed her, offering her a month's wages. Grace was not expecting to be given notice and did not take it very well. She was a greedy woman who liked to spend money as fast as she got it, and she really expected that she would stay on in some other role, having developed romantic feelings for her boss. "Can I please stay on in another position," asked Grace. "No, you will only remind me of my babies, it is better that you leave," said Richard firmly. Grace left the room slamming the door behind her.

Later that day Richard received a visit from Dr Brown to see how he was coping. "Not very well," said Richard sadly. "have to bury my babies tomorrow and I don't know how I will ever manage without my little babies." Dr Brown talked to Richard for over an hour, telling him to take one day at a time and to get as much rest as he could. He suggested that Richard ride his horse each day and take a long walk as well. Richard agreed to do all of the things Dr Brown suggested. Dr Brown told Richard that Charlotte was clearly suffering from some kind of mental disorder, made much worse by the over indulgence of her parents Rupert and Priscilla Penfield.

The following day Richard attended the funeral service of his little boy and girl, held at the same church where they were baptised. He was really glad that they were baptised, knowing that they were part of God's family made him feel a little better. The service was attended by all of his servants, a few neighbours and friends and at the back of the church one lone woman, dressed in black with a black bonnet and veil covering her face. That woman was Molly. Grace did not attend which Richard found strange, since she had looked after the babies from birth. Charlotte was buried in another area of the churchyard reserved for paupers. Her parents did not attend her service. Richard looked for the woman in black after the service but she was nowhere to be found. One of his servants thought she may have been the woman who had found his wife and twins. Following the funeral and the small wake afterwards, Richard donated all of the twins' belongings including toys and clothes to the thrift shop. He asked the servants to take all of Charlotte's clothes and belongings onto the front lawn where he made a huge bonfire and burnt the lot. Her room was redecorated with new paint, wallpaper and carpet rugs. He wanted no reminder of his wife or what she had done.

Richard tried to do as Dr Brown suggested and on another visit to his home Dr Brown asked Richard how he was doing "You have lost weight Richard and you look tired," said Dr Brown, concerned. "I have not been sleeping well. The house is like a morgue and I cannot concentrate on anything in my work," replied Richard. "My life will never be the same without my children," he said. "Have you considered taking a trip back to England to visit your family?" asked Dr Brown. "Well as a matter of fact, I have been thinking about it," said Richard as they sat down for a cup of tea together.

A few weeks later Richard set sail on board "The New Horizon" for London to visit his family in England. The trip was very rough and many people were seasick. Richard managed to stay on his feet, but was extremely relieved when the ship docked. His father was waiting with a carriage to take him to their country home just outside London. In the warmth of his family's love and caring, Richard instantly knew that he had done the right thing in returning to England.

Richard and his father took long walks around the large estate and went riding each day. He had lovely friendly chats with his young sister Emily who by now had grown into a beautiful young woman and his quiet gentle mother who had a way of calming him and just by her very presence inspiring him to be more positive. He and his father went to the library each evening and had a glass of port while they discussed politics and world problems. Richard was happy with his family, their love and support went a long way to help him to grieve the loss of his children. "Father, I still have not forgotten my brother's drowning. The death of my twins brought it all back to me," said Richard. His father replied, "my son, I know you blamed yourself for your brother's death, but I assure you, it was an accident, pure and simple, and you must not dwell on it." "You must try to move on with your life. You are still a young man and might fall in love one day." Richard shook his head at the last remark. A few weeks later Richard decided to return to Australia. He needed to attend to his business there and also look after his sheep and cattle once more. The trip home

was not as bumpy as the one on the way over and a few weeks later Richard arrived back at his home "Darley Park".

His servants were delighted to see him home and especially his groom and favourite horse Albie. The cook prepared his favourite meal of roast lamb with mint sauce and roast vegetables and bread and butter pudding with cream all served with wine from one of his wineries, a new venture for Richard. He walked around his lovely property and for the first time felt a feeling of hope. The healing had begun.

11

Grace Jones

Grace Jones had come to Australia with her husband William Jones who wanted to get rich by searching for gold. William was a tall, dark, handsome man with a lot of charisma and Grace was besotted with him when she first met him in England. Grace had grown up with wealth. Her father had inherited money from his grandmother but unfortunately he was a gambler, playing cards and going to the horse races and before long the comfortable life which the family once knew was gone, as one by one valuable paintings and jewels were sold off to pay his gambling debts. Grace bitterly resented her new status as a pauper and when William proposed she gladly accepted, keen to follow him to Australia with the promise of gold.

William did find gold when he first came to Australia and Grace and her young daughter Isabel were well provided for until illness struck both William and Isabel and they both died of Whooping Cough. With William's death, Grace was left with little money and needed to work. The job as nanny to the

Darley twins came at exactly the right time for Grace. The pay was good and it was not difficult work because the many servants assisted her so much. Grace was a big spender. She liked to spend her money on boiled lollies and penny dreadfuls, never on anything useful like proper food. At the Darley home, Grace had all of her meals so she did not have to buy food. Grace was not a very attractive woman. Her appearance was not helped by the fact that she was overweight from eating so many sweet foods like cakes and jellies.

When the twins died, Grace at first was relieved. They were starting to be a lot more work since they had begun to crawl and stand up. When Richard terminated her services she was stunned. She truly believed that he would let her remain at the home in some other capacity. She even thought that he might make her his new bride, but Richard almost threw her out of the house and Grace was furious. "How dare he treat her like a servant after she had practically raised his two babies," she said to herself, full of anger and resentment.

Grace faced the fact that she would need to work again after her four weeks' pay quickly ran out. She had no idea about saving. She went to the employment office to find work and fortunately Molly had only just been there to see if she could get a nanny for some help for her now very busy twins. Grace was directed to the boarding house where Ben and Molly interviewed her in the Library. "Come and meet the twins," said Molly. Grace followed Molly into the nursery where on seeing the twins Grace let out a gasp "Oh my goodness," she said. "What is wrong Grace?" asked Molly. "Oh, nothing, they are just so beautiful," replied Grace who could hardly believe the resemblance of Molly's twins to the twins she had just worked with. Not only that but Molly Chandler was identical to the wife of her previous employer, Charlotte Darley. Grace wondered if it was possible that they could have been twins. "Is Ben the children's father?" asked Grace with suspicion in her voice. "Of course he is, why would you even ask such a thing," replied Molly, not at all happy with Grace's personal question. From that moment on, Molly felt uncomfortable with Grace and did not trust her. She wished then that they had not employed her.

Grace started work the next day, working four days a week. She found the twins very active and tiring as they were very busy. She had to work this time because Molly and Ben were always around watching her and keeping an eye on the children. She had lunch and dinner with the family and was given a good wage, but still managed to be always short of money. She approached Molly one day to try to get more money in her wages. Molly said she would discuss it with Ben.

In the meantime Molly asked some of her friends what they paid their nannies and found that she was actually paying Grace far more than was the norm. She decided to make a visit to the home of Mr Darley to see if his housekeeper knew what they had paid Grace when she worked at "Darley House". The housekeeper, Mrs Williams and the cook, Mrs Robson invited Molly to take tea with them. They told Molly that she was paying Grace far more than she had received at "Darley House". "You need to keep an eye on that one," said Mrs Williams. "Why do you say that?" asked Molly. "Well she was sneaky, always trying to get other people to mind the twins and chasing after the master," said Mrs Robson. Molly left the ladies then, now feeling even more unsure about having employed Grace. When she told Ben he suggested that they cut her hours back and then after a while dismiss her. Molly didn't really like Grace very much and she usually liked everyone.

Molly told Grace that they believed that they were already paying her too much and that they would only need her two days a week. Grace took it very badly and left the room slamming the door behind her. The weeks turned to months and the twins grew up fast, both now walking and having past their first birthday. It was celebrated with a cake and lots of home -made ice cream and naturally they both needed a bath afterwards. They were lovely looking children with their golden curls and beautiful blue eyes. They were also beautiful inside as well, both having sweet gentle natures like their mother. They did manage to get into a lot of mischief, much to Grace's dislike as she needed to bath them when they made mud pies or played with the chooks.

Molly and Ben did not trust Grace, so they insisted on taking the twins for their daily walks, saying it was exercise for them. This annoyed Grace who wanted the easy jobs, not the dirty jobs like bathing the twins when they were dirty. In reality Grace hated her job, just as she had begun to hate her job with the Darley twins. She was not a maternal person, being much too selfish to care about anyone else.

Grace wandered around the house doing as little as possible with a scowl on her face. Molly and Ben no longer felt that they needed Grace and were unhappy with her negative attitude feeling it was bad for the twins. They wanted them to be around cheerful people. Ben called Grace into the library and told her that they would no longer need her services, giving her two weeks' pay. As expected Grace took it badly, standing up and hurling abuse at Ben, then walking out, slamming the door behind her. Molly was really glad when she left, never feeling comfortable when she was around.

Grace had no home and no job. The two week's pay was gone in two days. She remembered an old mate Jim Connor, whom she met one day, when she caught him breaking into a house she was working at and did not give him away to the police. Jim owed her, so she thought. She found his house which was a shanty at the edge of town and knocked on the door. Lucky for her Jim was home and reluctantly invited her in. "I need somewhere to stay Jim," she said. "I have lost my job and have no money," she added. "Okay, you can stay for a while, but not too long," said Jim. Jim did not like Grace much, but she knew about his petty thieving and could tell the police at any time. Jim had been a petty thief in England and was transported to Australia as a convict for theft. In Australia he continued his thieving, stealing from the wealthy in Ballarat and selling his loot in Melbourne. He also had managed to find some gold as well, so had a comfortable income, not that he told Grace.

Grace spent her days lying on the sofa, reading her penny dreadfuls, eating boiled lollies and plotting in her mind how she could get back at Ben and Molly for their treatment of her. She came up with a plan which she discussed with Jim when he returned one night from a robbbery. At first Jim was not interested and told her so, but she threatened to turn him in, so he had no choice but to go along with her. "You won't have to do much Jim, I will do it all," said Grace. She decided to burn the boarding house, not badly, just enough to scare them. Grace went to the general store disguised as a man and bought several cans of kerosene. She cut up old rags which she found in Jim's shed and waited until the time was right. She still had a key to the back door of the boarding house, never having handed it back to Molly. Jim's role in the plot was to set fire to the kerosene soaked rags throughout the bottom floor.

Fire

One rainy night a few weeks later Grace decided the time was right to carry out her plan. Jim was reluctant at first but Grace kept reminding him of what she would do and since he really believed that she would turn him in, he obeyed her. Jim was a weak spineless man who had been married with children in England whom he never thought about. He set off in the rain to start the evil deed. Grace decided to stay home and let Jim take the blame if he was caught. He used the key to get into the house through the back door. The house was silent with the entire household asleep upstairs, guests and all. He spread out all of the fuel soaked rags throughout the entire lower floor and lit the one closest to the back door through which he made a quick exit. Jim went across the road and hit beneath a verandah post of an old darkened shop to watch the fire progress.

Molly woke up to the smell of smoke. She quickly ran to Ben's room and alerted him. Ben went immediately to the twins' room and took the twins down the back stairs with Molly. They then alerted all of the guests and Ben worked quickly and tirelessly to get each and every guest and servant out as the flames licked up the sides of the boarding house and thick smoke bellowed out from the inside of the house. People began to gather outside, joining the boarding house guests who were in their nightclothes and were huddled together, confused and upset. Molly stood with them, frightened and worried. She had not seen Ben for over half an hour. She asked everyone she saw "Have you seen Ben, do you know where he is?"

The fire carts arrived and started to put out the fire. It was a savage fire and took ages to put out. Molly was starting to get very concerned for Ben's safety. Eventually the firemen brought out two bodies on makeshift trolleys. Molly raced over and looked at the bodies. They were both badly burnt but she recognised Ben's torn shirt and one slipper. She knelt down and kissed his burnt face, praying over his body "My dearest Ben, you have been the most wonderful father and husband and I now pray to God to take you in his arms to be with him in heaven. I will never forget you, my love."

Molly was taken away by one of the guests who said, "Come away dear, there is nothing you can do now. You are in shock and need to be with your babies." Molly allowed herself to be moved away from the two burnt bodies and back to her children whom she hugged tightly, never wanting to ever let them go. Over the road Jim watched with glee as the fire took hold. He went home and told Grace that the place had burnt to the ground. Grace was very excited and demanded that Jim tell her every little part of the huge fire incident. As he spoke Grace rubbed her hands together with joy. She saw the evil deed as a huge success.

Back at the scene of the fire Molly was taken in by the couple who ran an Inn further out of town. They were a lovely couple named Mavis and Ian Bennet who had a grown up family. They took charge of Molly and her twins, giving them clothes to wear and beds to sleep in. Molly wanted to have the twins sleep in the same room as her. She was terrified that something would happen to them. Dr Brown came and gave Molly a sleeping potion. He told Mavis that Molly was in shock and needed rest and quiet. Mavis and Ian looked after Molly, organising the guests who had been staying at the boarding house and arranging for the funeral home to come to visit Molly to discuss Ben's funeral. The minister who baptised the twins also called and discussed the funeral service. Molly knew that Ben would want a simple service and to be buried with his first wife whom he had loved so much.

The twins wanted their father and walked around calling his name "dada, dada, where are you," they would call. Molly could not make them understand that their father had gone to heaven as they were too young to understand. She herself did not understand why her husband had died. She knew that he had gone into the boarding house one last time to see if anyone was still inside and had been caught by a falling piece of timber, but did not understand why God had taken such a lovely man to his home.

The day of the funeral arrived. Molly was dressed in a black outfit belonging to Mavis Bennet who watched the twins while Molly attended the funeral. The service was simple but appropriate with the minister describing Ben as an honest hardworking man with a gentle caring nature, a loving husband and father. Molly could not hold back her tears and sobbed uncontrollably throughout the service and burial. Afterwards a small wake was held in the supper room attached to the church. The funeral was well attended by townspeople, as Ben was well liked in the community.

Molly returned to the inn and confided in Mavis "I don't know how I will ever manage without Ben. Not only was he a wonderful father and helped me with the twins but the boarding house was our living and now I have no money and two children to raise alone," Molly said sadly. Mavis told her to go to bed and rest and that something would turn up. "Just pray about it dear," said Mavis softly.

A few days after the funeral Molly was resting in the afternoon while Mavis watched the twins when she had a knock on her door. Mavis informed her that a lawyer had come and wished to see her, "I really can't be bothered with him at the moment," said Molly. Mavis replied "I think you should see him my dear, it might be important." Molly nodded and tidied herself to go downstairs to meet with the lawyer. His name was Mr Moore and he was a middle aged man, rather on the portly side with a long beard and thick moustache. He was seated in the sitting room of the inn talking to Ian Bennet and stood up when Molly arrived. Ian excused himself and left her alone with Mr Moore.

"How are you Mrs Chandler?" he asked politely. "Well I have seen better days," Molly replied. "Are you aware that Ben made a new will about a year ago my dear?" asked Mr Moore. Molly said she had no idea as Ben had not told her about any will. "Well after the twins were born he wanted to make provision for them and yourself and so he made a new will leaving all his possessions including shares, gold leases, property in England and family jewels to you Mrs Molly Chandler," said Mr Moore. "But I thought that Ben's only asset was the boarding house which has now gone," said Molly. "No my dear, Ben was a very wealthy man, having been left a large inheritance from his maternal grandmother as well. You will be one of the wealthiest people in the country." Molly could hardly believe what she was hearing. She had absolutely no idea that Ben was a wealthy man. He lived a simple life but always insisted in having the best food and clothing for his family. Molly always thought that the income from the boarding house was a good one and indeed it was, especially since Molly became the cook. In her prayers that night, silently Molly thanked Ben for his provision for her and the twins. She was so glad that Ben experienced fatherhood with her children before he died. What a truly amazing man he really was.

PART

Three

CHAPTER

13

Murder

As usual, Grace needed money. Jim was out a lot seeking gold and selling it. He allowed Grace to stay and provided food and shelter, but he would not give her cash, knowing she would only spend it on rubbish. Lying on the couch, brooding and angry, Grace came up with another plan. This time she decided that they would steal from the wealthy homes in Ballarat. Once again Grace threatened poor weak Jim into submission to perform another illegal act. Jim drank at a local pub and played cards with one of the servants from the Penfield house. Grace told Jim to keep the rum flowing to the man in order to get information about the house and how to get in. The poor man became very talkative when plied with the rum and even drew a mud map for Jim. He told Jim that the scullery door was always left unlocked and where Mrs Penfield kept her jewels. He also told Jim where the best silver was kept.

Grace made up a disguise to cover her hair and face, wearing trousers to look like a man. Jim also wore dark clothes including a dark coat and hat. They found out from Jim's mate, that the Penfields were going away the following weekend so decided to execute their plan then. On the Saturday morning in question, Priscilla Penfield woke with a bad cold. The doctor was called and she was told to remain in bed for a few days. He ordered a nurse to stay at the house to relieve the housekeeper and cook who were getting on a bit in age and Priscilla was a demanding patient constantly calling for things all day and night.

Grace and Jim were unaware of the Penfields' change of plans and set out to "Seven Oaks" following the mud map given to Jim. They entered through the scullery door and quickly and silently went upstairs to find the jewels. Grace was covered top to toe in black and looked even larger than she was. She went to Priscilla's bedroom first while Jim looked in the drawers in Rupert's room. As she was going through the drawers in Priscilla's cupboard, Priscilla suddenly turned in her bed, hearing a rustling noise in her room. She called for her nurse, but the nurse had gone downstairs to make a drink of hot milk and all Priscilla could see was a large dark shape near her cupboard. "Rupert, Rupert, come quickly," she screamed. Rupert hearing her call and spotting Jim in the shadows of his room ran quickly to his wife. "Robbers, Robbers," she said to Rupert. Jim reacted, knowing that he had been seen and possibly recognised in the half light of the room. He took his weapon from its holster, shooting both Rupert and Priscilla in the chest as they huddled together in fright in the hall. Both of them fell to the floor instantly. Grace gathered as much jewellery as she could into her bag and Jim started down the stairs to get the silver. As he went into the dining room, Mrs Beale and Mrs Banks, having heard the shots came running into the downstairs hallway in their nightgowns. Jim once again aware that they could recognise him, used his weapon again and pointed it at both ladies, shooting both of them. The ladies fell to the floor in a pool of blood as Jim and Grace hurried out of the house to where their horses were tied up just a few yards away from the main house. They raced to their home where they laughed with joy as they unpacked their spoils from the evening's work. Jim felt no remorse at having shot four people, neither did Grace, in fact it made her feel excited. Prior to going to the robbery Grace had insisted that Jim take a knife and his rifle just in case they were caught in the act. He was reluctant at first but realised that it would be the best thing to do. They definitely did not want to be recognised.

Meanwhile back at "Seven Oaks", the nurse who had been hiding in a cupboard, came out sobbing uncontrollably to find the two ladies lying where they had fallen. She bent over them and discovered that Mrs Beale was dead but Mrs Banks still had a pulse. She ran from the house to find one of the grooms who slept in a hut behind the main house. He then rode his horse to get police and ambulance cart to hurry to the house. Before long there were a large number of people in the house. Mr and Mrs Penfield and Mrs Beale were taken away by the funeral director in his cart and Mrs Banks was taken to the hospital in the ambulance cart. The doctor had been and examined her. It appeared that her wound was not too deep and she would most likely survive, although she was suffering from shock. All she could tell the police was that one of the men was very large and was dressed all in black. The other man was slim and had a small beard. He was not very tall and he was wearing a long black coat and a hat.

The police searched the house and grounds all night and the next day. They found evidence of where horses had been tied up and lolly wrappers nearby. It appeared to be a robbery gone wrong. The servants spent the day cleaning the floors, They were deeply saddened by Mrs Beale's death and grateful that Mrs Banks had survived. Since they had little to do with the Penfields, they did not mourn them in the same way. Mrs Beale was buried from her church three days later and the service was well attended. The Penfields were cremated and out of respect, the servants attended a brief service which took only ten minutes.

The police tried to trace family of the Penfields but could find no immediate family in Australia or England. With the death of their daughter and grandchildren, there was no immediate kin, so the entire estate passed to distant cousins living in Melbourne. The cousins were keen to sell the house as soon as possible in order to get the money from the sale. Agents appointed to sell the house felt that a good price could not be forthcoming because of the murders that had taken place there. The house had recently been remodelled, with the two upper bedrooms completely repainted with new curtains and floor coverings. The hallways and kitchen areas where the shooting took place were renovated. The house presented for sale now looked immaculate. All it needed was a buyer to love it and make it a happy home. It had never really been a happy home, although during the past couple of years it had improved with the marriage of Charlotte to Mr Richard Darley.

The police continued to search for evidence to solve the murders of the three people at "Seven Oaks". Their search took them to the Ballarat general store where they were told by the owner that a large woman possibly posing as a man in dark clothing with her face covered, had purchased several tins of kerosene just before the boarding house fire. They started to put together a case in which they believed the two incidents could be connected. What was confusing them was whether the person in the dark clothing was a man or a woman. They were determined to solve the two cases.

A New Beginning

I n the meantime, **Molly and her two children who were still staying at the inn with Mavis and** Ian, were slowly coming to terms with the death of Ben. It was hard for them at first, especially for the twins who missed their father very much. Molly was having trouble adjusting to being a woman of wealth. The most important thing on her agenda at the moment was to find a permanent home for them all to live in. She made contact with the agent in Ballarat to find them a home, Her requirements were that the house be large with a big garden, not too far from the main town area, with two floors and a big room on the ground floor to be used as a playroom for the twins.

Mr Telford, the agent came to Molly and said he had found the perfect house. "There is a problem, however. The house known as "Seven Oaks" was the scene of a triple murder just recently and many people have negative feelings about living in such a house," said Mr Telford. Molly told him that she knew the house, although she had never been past the kitchen area. She said, "I don't have a problem with the murders. The house has nothing to do with that." Mr Telford arranged for Molly to view the house the next day. He told her that it was a really good price because the distant cousins wanted it sold as soon as possible in order to get the cash.

The following day Molly went back to "Seven Oaks" with Mr Telford, this time entering through the front door. The entrance and foyer were beautiful, looking down on them was a magnificent crystal chandelier. Molly fell in love with the house immediately. What she loved most was a huge room close to the kitchen and dining room which would make a great playroom for the twins. Upstairs, the entire floor had been refurbished and the bedrooms were tastefully furnished. Molly would only need to outfit the nursery in colours and wallpaper suitable for young children. Otherwise the house was perfect. Molly negotiated a good price and arranged to move in within two weeks.

Two weeks later Molly moved in to her new home with all new furniture purchased from the large department store in Ballarat, along with all new toys and clothes for all of them. Some of the servants stayed on but Molly was more comfortable with new people after being a convict in the same house a few years ago. She had a forgiving nature, but she could not forget how some of the servants treated her when she worked in the scullery. Molly changed the name of the house. It was now to be known as "Chandler House". A new cook was needed. Molly found out the Mrs Banks was still in the hospital so she decided to pay her a visit.

Mrs Banks had survived the murder attempt but was still very upset by the death of her friend Mrs Beale, whom she had worked with for many years. She remained in the hospital as her recovery was slow. She welcomed a visit from Molly one day out of the blue. "Molly, how lovely to see you. You look so beautiful and mature. Tell me what you have been doing," said Mrs Banks. Molly told her of her work at the boarding house, her marriage to Ben, the birth of her twins and the fire which killed her husband. "Mrs Banks, would you like to come back to work for me. I have bought "Seven Oaks", but it is called "Chandler House" now, and I need a cook. I will of course be working in the kitchen with you so you can work as many hours as you feel you can manage?" asked Molly. Mrs Banks was delighted to be asked to come back to work again. "Thank you Molly, I think work might be just what I need to get me out of this depression I now feel since the attack. I know I am lucky to be alive, but I have been struggling of late," said Mrs Banks. Molly asked Mrs Banks if she knew of a suitable person to be a nanny for her twins. Mrs Banks said her daughter in law Judy was a wonderful mother and her two children had grown up and left home so she felt sure that she would love a job of caring for little ones again. Molly left the hospital then, after telling Mrs Banks that she would have a room ready for her if she wished to live with the family.

Judy Banks came for an interview and Molly liked her instantly. She started work straight away and the twins liked her as well. She was kind and gentle and her ideas on child raising were similar to those of Molly. The large playroom on the ground floor was wonderful especially if the weather was poor. Judy and the twins spent a lot of time outside, feeding the ducks in the pond or gathering eggs from the hen house which Molly started years ago as a convict. They took long walks in their baby carriage, enjoying the sights and sounds of the native bushland.

Back at Jim's shanty, Grace was bored. Jim had gone off to Melbourne to sell some of the stolen jewels and silverware from the Penfield robbery, leaving Grace with plenty of food, but she craved more excitement and action in her life. She decided to try to get a job in a rich person's home where she could attempt to steal in a small way. Her first position as a nanny, was in a house with three boys. The home was chaotic and Grace did not care about the mess. The boys were little horrors and tried every trick in the book to upset Grace. She lasted there three weeks after the father came home and found Grace smacking the youngest boy on the bottom. Her next position was with a family with six children where Grace was expected to cook, clean and wash clothes, in short she had to work. She hated it so much, but kept going for six weeks until she finally gave in and left. She decided then to try her hand at being a maid in a wealthy home since she could not get many jewels when she was surrounded by children. She took a job in another wealthy home as a maid, this time she did not have to mind children. Grace could not help herself. She liked pretty things and had managed to persuade Jim to allow her to keep a beautiful diamond bracelet which was part of a set, after the Penfield murders. They did not get the necklace or the earrings, much to Grace's disgust, but the bracelet was now hers and she wore it everywhere, telling people it belonged to her grandmother.

Molly decided to clear out a davenport desk which had remained in Priscilla's bedroom. It had lots of little drawers in which Priscilla hid papers and sometimes special jewels. Molly found a diamond necklace and earrings. It appeared to be a set but without the bracelet. She decided to keep it and wear it at appropriate times. Tucked in another drawer were papers which when spread out, indicated the adoption of Charlotte Duffy by Mr and Mrs Penfield in England over twenty six years ago. Molly stared at the papers. She was not surprised at what she saw, just saddened. She wondered if her sister's behaviour may have been better if she had a sister to confide in. From what Dr Brown said, Charlotte had a mental disorder and nothing would have helped her. Even so, Molly would have enjoyed knowing her sister.

When the twins had turned two and Judy was very comfortable in the house with them Molly decided to take passage back to England to see if her mother and brother were still alive. She felt that it had been many years since she had last seen them and she had doubts as to whether she could even find them let alone find them alive. She arranged to take passage to England the following week when a ship was leaving for Europe.

Molly left the country as a wealthy widow taking first class passage and sitting at the captain's table for dinner. She tried to forget her trip over to Australia in the bottom of the ship in overcrowded filthy conditions, and began to focus on her task of finding her mother and brother. The trip over was uneventful. Molly made friends with one of the other ladies returning to nurse her sick mother. "It is hard being so far from family," said Eve, her new friend. "Yes I know what you mean," replied Molly. "I have not seen my mother for many years and do not know if she is still living," she said sadly. "Where do you plan to start Molly?" asked Eve. "I think I will start back in London where I last saw my mother and brother. I doubt if they will still be in the same house, but someone might know where they have moved to or if they have passed away," said Molly seriously.

The ship docked in England at last. Molly hardly recognised London. She was only a young girl of sixteen when she last saw the big city and now she had returned as a wealthy widow and the mother of two children, much more mature and aware of the world around her. She booked into one of London's best hotels with a two bedroom suite at her disposal, having her own maid attached to the suite. The maid organised her unpacking while Molly went downstairs to see the bell captain.

She asked him if he could recommend a suitable person to assist her in finding her mother and brother. "I need a strong man, one who knows the poorer areas of London well and is not bothered about searching in those areas," Molly said. The bell captain said he would contact a few people he knew and let her know shortly. In the meantime, Molly moved into the dining room and had a delicious meal of roast beef, Yorkshire pudding and roast vegetables, followed by apple pie and custard. Feeling comfortable and replenished Molly went to her room for a rest.

Later that day a message came from the bell captain to say that he had found a suitable man to accompany her on her quest to find her family. He would be available in two days' time to start the search with her. Molly was delighted. She spent the next two days shopping in London at the best stores. She bought new clothes for the twins who were growing like mushrooms, in larger sizes as well. She indulged herself as well, purchasing some charming gowns and bonnets that she planned to wear when she went back to Australia. She bought gifts for Mrs Banks and Judy, lovely cashmere scarves and gloves to match as well as pure silk stockings for both of them. Her wonderful shopping spree over, Molly returned to the hotel to prepare for her next day and her meeting with Joe Martin, the man who was to become her constant companion for the next few days or weeks.

15

The Search

The next day Joe Martin arrived in his carriage to start the search. Molly was introduced to a very large, tall dark skinned man named Joe. Molly explained to Joe where she had last seen her parents, so they went immediately to her old home. It was in a poorer area of London, but not too difficult to find. Molly went in to her old home and found total strangers living there which did not surprise her. Unfortunately they had no knowledge of the folk who had lived there before them. Molly asked around at various neighbours, only to find that they had either moved on or died. On the first day of the search it seemed that they had absolutely no luck at all.

The following day Molly decided to go to other parts of London ever poorer than the day before. They looked up and down cobbled streets, went through burnt out houses and knocked on doors of old rental properties. Joe Martin was a big strong man who did not seem to mind walking through sewerage and filth. He had spent a lot of time in Boxing tents as a lad, making money and now worked as an investor. He was very comfortable and could afford to pick and choose his work. His job with Molly intrigued him.

Another two days passed with no luck at all. On the fourth day Molly was talking to an old man with a small sack walking down a small laneway. "What do you have in your sack?" she asked him. "Just a few bits and pieces from the river," the old man said under his breath "I'm a mudlark, missy," he said. He told her that most of the mudlarks lived in one area so that they could be close to their work. They usually worked from Vauxhall Bridge, eastwards to Blackwall on the north bank and Woolwich on the south. The mudlarks were scavengers who worked in London's river Thames when tides were low, among the vessels. They scratched a living by searching for things like coal, bits of old iron, bones, copper or nails, in the foul smelling mud and sewerage. There they would find the scraps that fell from the ships being repaired or out of service, making a small living.

This piece of news was the only clue so far for Joe and Molly to follow. At least they had an area to search and it was possible that her mother and Philip had become mudlarks. Realising that it was only a possibility, Molly and Joe went to the area which the old man mentioned. Once there, they asked about a woman and a cripple. Most of the people shook their heads, frightened of police or anyone else suspicious. At last one woman, old and frail, said that she had seen the cripple a few times and indicated the place where she had seen him. Molly and Joe then started to knock on doors, where there were any. The area was full of flea ridden, revolting slums, housing dozens of homeless people, all huddled together like animals in large rooms. Hygiene was non - existent for the poor souls.

Eventually they came upon one such room and Molly peeped inside. She looked in the corner and thought she recognised Philip's walking cane. Going over towards him she saw an old woman dressed in rags, her hair dirty and slimy, hanging down her back. There was no doubt about it, that woman was Sarah Duffy. Molly made her way to the woman calling out to her "Mother, Mother, it is I, Molly, I am here." Molly ran towards her mother who stood up and looked at the beautiful woman before her in disbelief. "Oh my God, I don't believe it, Molly, my beautiful Molly, you are here," Sarah said sobbing as she hugged her daughter as if she never wanted to let her go. Philip gazed in wonder at his younger sister, tears streaming down his poor dirty face. Molly introduced Joe to her family and hurried to get them out of the horrible place in which they were living. They went with Molly in Joe's carriage which took them back to the hotel by the back entrance, leading them up the servants' stairs to avoid any embarrassment for Molly and her family. Once in her suite Molly asked her maid to organise hot baths for her mother and brother, bathing them both in lavender water and washing their hair with sweet smelling soap. Molly noticed that they were both painfully thin and sent for sandwiches and tea for them all. While they were eating she paid Joe a fee much more than he had asked. He thanked her, saying how much he had enjoyed their adventure together.

Molly left her mother and brother to rest in another room which she had booked and went once more to the shops to purchase clothes for them both. She bought gowns, bonnets, boots, stockings, gloves, nighties and underwear for her mother and shirts, pants, jumpers, underwear, pyjamas, boots, hats, gloves and scarves for Philip. She also purchased personal items like hairbrushes and combs, having all of the items delivered to the hotel immediately.

After Philip and Sarah had their rest the items arrived and they both commenced a fashion parade, trying on every outfit for Molly to inspect. She was delighted to see the happiness on their faces. "Molly darling, we never expected to ever see you again, and now here you are, alive and well and not only that, but a wealthy widow and the mother of two children. How wonderful is that," said Sarah.

Molly quickly organised for the three of them to return to Australia on the next ship leaving London, just a week away. When they left for the ship both Sarah and Philip were both looking much better after a week of beautiful food. Philip was very excited to be going on a large vessel, while Sarah was just happy to be reunited with her family. Before leaving Molly arranged for a plaque to be placed on her father's grave. It said -

> In loving memory of Benjamin Duffy
> Loved and loving husband of Sarah
> Devoted father of Philip and Molly
> Never Forgotten

The family left England on the ship "Mornington" on a dull English day. They were first class passengers and for Sarah the experience was wonderful. Philip loved being on deck talking to the sailors. Molly was just anxious to get home to her children and to see how much they had grown during her time away.

The ship docked in Melbourne a few weeks later and Molly and her mother and brother, both looking much healthier after a taste of sea air and good food, left Melbourne by coach for their home in Ballarat. Sarah stepped out of the carriage and gazed in amazement at the beautiful home standing before her. "Oh Molly, It is so magnificent, I can hardly believe your good fortune," said Sarah as she entered the front door leading into the foyer with its gorgeous chandelier hanging from the ceiling. Laughter could be heard as the twins ran to their mother. "Mama, mama, come here,|" they said as they threw themselves into Molly's waiting arms.

"Why Molly, you did not tell me they were twins," said Sarah in surprise. Molly replied, "I wanted to surprise you mother." "What beautiful children," added Sarah. "Meet Sarah Emily and Richard Benjamin," said Molly proudly introducing the twins to her mother and brother. Now over two, the twins were enchanting and had grown considerably since Molly had been away. Molly found Mrs Banks and Jenny Banks and they all went into the playroom to look at the new toys and clothes. The gifts for the two ladies were received with delight by the two ladies.

Molly took her mother and brother to their rooms to rest and sat down with

Jenny and Mrs Banks to find out what had been happening in the town since she had left. "Well there have been a lot of robberies since you left, The police are looking for two people, one a large man or woman and the other a slim middle aged man, but no arrests have yet been made," said Mrs Banks.

Sarah and Philip soon fitted into the family life at "Chandler House" as if they had lived there all their lives. Sarah was able to help Mrs Banks in the kitchen and Philip loved to work outside with the horses and grooms. Molly started to make friends with other mothers at her local church group and they had play times at various houses. Her best friend was Mabel Donald who lived in a large house not far from Molly. Mabel had two children aged two and 3 and loved to visit Molly with her big playroom. Molly in turn enjoyed going to Mabel's place where there were lots of animals for the children to play with. One day Molly came in the back door and noticed a bracelet sitting on the side table in the scullery. It looked to be diamond. In fact it looked identical to Molly's incomplete set in her home. She asked Mabel, "who owns that bracelet Mabel?" To which Mabel replied "It belongs to our maid, Grace Jones, why do you ask?" Molly told her what she knew and Mabel said that they had noticed some things missing from her cupboards, like jewels and silverware. The women agreed to be careful of Grace and Mabel decided to go to the Police and tell them what she knew.

Mabel attended the police station the next day and told them what she knew, about the bracelet and what Molly told her about Grace's time as a nanny to Sarah and Ritchie. They took down notes and told her that they were already watching Grace and her partner Jim. When she left, the two policemen discussed the two cases, now firmly convinced that this couple was responsible for all five murders which included Ben and the guest he had tried to save. Mabel's description of Grace Jones, that she was a rather large woman also led them to believe that Grace was indeed a person of very much interest.

16

Ben's Place

Molly still owned the land on which had stood her and Ben's boarding house. She had the rubble cleared and asked an architect to look into the possibility of rebuilding the boarding house on the same spot and in a similar manner. He got back to her and presented her with the plans. She made contact with a builder and decided to rebuild the boarding house, starting as soon as possible. Her plan was to put her mother Sarah in charge to run the boarding house and there would be work for Philip there as well. When she put the idea to her mother, Sarah was at first reluctant, lacking confidence but Molly talked her into it and soon Sarah was helping Molly with the planning, picking out fabrics for curtains, rugs and crockery and cutlery to go in the new boarding house.

Soon it was built and Philip started a simple garden at the front, as well as a vegetable garden at the back. Molly and Sarah interviewed servants as well as an assistant cook for Sarah. The new place was to be called "Ben's Place" in honour of the man who gave his life to save others in the fire which destroyed his home and family life.

Sarah and Philip moved over to the boarding house to live. Although sad to see them go Molly made sure that the twins saw their grandmother and uncle regularly.

Before too long the boarding house was in full swing and Sarah found that she could manage with ease even when the place filled up. Philip was in his element working with the grooms and horses and being the odd job man and gardener at the boarding house, giving him a feeling of being worthwhile for the first time in his life.

One day when Jenny Banks was out walking with the twins in their baby carriage a stranger stopped to say hello. He looked into the baby carriage and got the shock of his life. The twins were exactly the same as his own two dead babies except that they were older. He could hardly believe what he was seeing. "Who are these children?" he asked Jenny. Jenny was a bit reluctant to talk to him until he said, "I am Richard Darley, of "Darley House", just near here, I will not harm you." Jenny then said, "They are the children of Molly Chandler who is a widow and owns "Chandler House". Their names are Richard and Sarah Chandler." "Are they twins?" asked Richard. Jenny replied that they were indeed twins. "They are beautiful children," added Richard as he gazed at the two children so very similar to his own. Richard then went on his way, returning home where he pondered over the unbelievable likeness of the Chandler twins to his own now deceased babies.

Richard was determined to solve the mystery of the twins so he called at "Chandler House a few days later to see if he could meet Molly Chandler and unlock the story of the twins likeness to his own. Mrs Banks let him in and recognised him from her days working at "Seven Oaks".

"How are you Mrs Banks?" Richard asked, having heard about the terrible murders when he returned from England. "I am well sir," she replied. Richard asked to see Molly but Mrs Banks said she was out. He asked about the children and she took him to the playroom where Ritchie and Sarah were playing with dolls and a wooden truck. "What beautiful children they are," he said. "How old are they now Mrs Beale?" Mrs Beale told him they were nearly three Richard realised that his own twins would have been about the same age as these two, were they still living. He thanked her and said he would call again.

Richard went to his home and took a long ride on his favourite horse, needing to clear his head. He simply could not understand how those two children resembled his own two dead children so accurately. They were certainly beautiful children and from what he saw of them they were placid and well mannered. Their nanny seemed to be a sensible type of person too. The more he pondered the problem the more confused he became, so he went to bed and tried to sleep, not an easy thing to do with so many unanswered question twirling around in his head.

Kidnapped

Back at Jim's Shanty, Grace was moaning and groaning about having no money. Jim was heartily sick and tired of listening to her and told her he wanted her to leave. This did not go down very well with Grace who flew into a rage and started to threaten Jim. She told Jim they needed to get some serious money and she had a plan as to how they could do it. Her plan was to kidnap the Chandler twins and hold them until a ransom was paid. "I know we can pull it off Jim. That miss smarty pants, Molly Chandler gets around like the lady of the manor these days. She needs to be brought down a peg or two. We can take those two brats of hers that she adores so much and hide them until we get the ransom money. What do you think?" Jim was not in favour of the idea thinking it was too risky, but Grace was determined to do it, so he being the weakling that he was, had to agree in the end.

Grace set about making up ransom notes with cut outs from the local newspaper, She then looked around to find a vacant shed where she could hide the children. Eventually she came across a vacant shed at the back of an empty block of land at the end of a road. It looked as if no-one had been there for a long time. There were cobwebs all around the iron door and no sign of life. There was straw in the shed and she took water for the children to drink. The next part of her plan was to find a suitable drop off point for the money. She found an old red mailbox, perfect for a drop off. The mailbox was two streets away from Jim's shanty so she felt that it would be isolated enough for the purpose she had in mind.

Grace decided that she and Jim would get the children when they were on their daily walk with their nanny. She started watching the "Chandler House" and noted the time each day when Nanny Jenny took the twins for their walk. She followed them each day for a week, looking for a suitable place to intervene and take the children. She found the perfect place. It was a bend in the path, ideal for placing a large branch from a tree which the nanny would need to remove. While she was removing it, Grace and Jim would snatch the children and quickly take them on nearby horses to the shed Grace had found.

A sunny day the following week was the day Grace selected to kidnap the twins. She and Jim went to the place selected and placed a large branch from a gum tree at the spot they had chosen. Shortly after, Jenny arrived with the twins in their double baby carriage and as expected she left the twins and started to move the large branch from their path. Jim and Grace, wearing masks and dressed in dark clothing, quickly snatched the two children and on their horses raced away to the block of land containing the old shed. They placed the screaming children into the dark shed leaving them some bread and water and two blankets and left the shed after placing a padlock on the door. The poor little children lay huddled together on the straw supporting each other and crying, "Mama, mama."

During the night, Grace slipped one of the made up ransom notes under the front door of "Chandler House". By now the entire household was in despair as everyone searched the entire area and beyond for the missing children. Sarah and Philip arrived from the boarding house and the police were called. All local men joined in the search including Richard Darley. The police asked Molly who she thought might dislike her enough to do such a thing. The only person she could think of was Grace Jones. The police said that they were already watching her for other matters.

Molly was horrified when she received the ransom note the next morning. "My poor little children. They must be so frightened and hungry," she sobbed in her mother's arms.

The note said

LEAVE TWENTY THOUSAND POUNDS IN A RED MAIL BOX AT THE END OF GOLD TOWN ROAD. DO NOT GO TO POLICE. MONEY MUST BE PAID BY END OF WEEK OR CHILDREN WILL DIE.

Dr Brown was called to give Molly a sedative. The note was given to the police. Unbeknown to Molly the Police had a man watching Grace and Jim's shanty for any movement and also had another man watching the red mail box. One way or another they were determined to catch Grace Jones and her partner Jim.

A knock at the front door brought Richard Darley to "Chandler House". Mrs Banks invited him in and took him to the sitting room where Molly was sitting on her chaise lounge. Molly stood up and faced for the first time the father of her twins, the man with whom she had spent one memorable afternoon almost four years ago. Richard took Molly's hands and stood looking into her lovely blue eyes. "How beautiful you are Molly Chandler," said Richard as he looked deeply into her lovely blue eyes. Are you the woman with whom I shared a wonderful afternoon in a shed one rainy day about four years ago?" Yes, I am that woman," said Molly softly. "Are the twins mine?" Richard asked in a serious voice. "Yes Richard, they are," replied Molly quietly. Richard then took Molly in his arms, hugging her tightly as if he never wanted to let her go.

Richard asked Molly to tell him her story and so she did, telling him that she only found out for certain just a few months ago that Charlotte had been her twin sister. She told him that Ben had married her to give the babies a name and left her his fortune and that she suspected that Charlotte was her twin when she found her and the children at the river and saw the likeness to herself and the twins. "It is like a miracle. I have lost my twins and found new ones and now I have found you again, my lovely Molly. We need now to get our twins back. I have my entire household out searching and I am searching on horseback. I need to go now and speak to the Police. Try not to worry. We will find them my love."

Richard kissed her, then left to join the search. Meanwhile the man watching the red mail box reported back to his superior that a woman matching Grace's description was seen checking the mail box and was followed back to her shanty. Later that day, she left the shanty and was followed to an unused block of land containing an old shed which she entered and stayed for about five minutes.

Grace was furious when she went to the box and there was no money in it. She was sure that Molly would get the money straight away, not realising that Molly would need to wait until the bank opened. Later that day, she checked to see if the brats were still alive. She tossed a few scraps of bread and a couple of biscuits to the crying children, then locking the shed behind her, she took off on her horse back to her shanty. Shortly afterwards Richard, two of his servants and one of the policemen who had been watching the shed, broke open the lock and released the children, taking them swiftly to their home.

Richard knocked on the door of "Chandler House" where Molly was waiting, arms outstretched to receive her two beautiful children. Sarah and Philip raced to her side as all of them laughed and cried, welcoming home their brave little children. Mrs Banks immediately started making pancakes, their favourite meal and Jenny Banks could hardly contain her joy whom he had dreamed about for so long. At seeing her beloved charges back in their home again. Richard excused himself, promising to return the next day. He kissed Molly lightly on the cheek as he made his way to his horse.

Richard felt a surge of absolute joy as he went to his own home. Not only had he discovered that the two beautiful children were his, but their mother Molly was the lovely woman whom he had dreamed about for so many years. For the first time since the death of his twins he now had a future to look forward to.

The next day Grace went to the red mail box. Once again there was no money. Instead she was set upon by two large policemen who immediately arrested her on charges relating to kidnapping, robbery, arson and murder. Grace would not have to worry about where to live ever again because if she were not hanged then she would rot in goal for the rest of her life. Following the arrest of Grace, the police went looking for Jim but his shanty was empty and it seemed that he had moved on. The continued to look for him, but Jim remained as slippery as an eel and was never found.

The following day Richard arrived at "Chandler Place" for afternoon tea. The twins made him a pretend afternoon tea in their playroom and then he played with them and their blocks. Richard stayed for dinner. It was a celebration dinner with the best wine and the best silver. Mrs Banks made her famous Beef pot pies with potato mash and green beans followed by apple pie and fresh cream. Afterwards, Richard and Molly retired to the sitting room hand in hand. Molly was seated on the chaise lounge and Richard sat beside her. He asked her gently "Will you marry me Molly. I have loved since we first made love, all those years ago?" Molly could not hide her joy. "Yes Richard, Of course I will marry you. I love you too, and you are the father of my twins. I will never forget Ben and his kindness to me but the twins need a father in their lives and you will be just perfect." Ben kissed her deeply then before he took his leave.

Molly stood with Richard at the front door and as they looked at the sky they saw a double rainbow, just as they had on that special night four years ago.

THE END

EPILOGUE

Just one year later in the large master suite of "Chandler House", Richard and Sarah Chandler Darley welcomed their brother Andrew Richard and sister Anna Molly into their loving family. Their parents Richard and Molly Darley were thrilled to become parents again to another set of twins. Now a family of six, "Chandler House" was filled with laughter and love.

Printed in the United States
By Bookmasters